Marshall Cavendish Corporation, 99 White Plains Road, Tarrytown, New York 10591

www.marshallcavendish.us

Library of Congress Cataloging-in-Publication Data

Kimmel, Eric A.

The three cabritos / adapted by Eric A. Kimmel ; illustrated by Stephen Gilpin. — 1st ed.

p. cm.

Includes a Spanish-English glossary and pronunciation guide.

Summary: Retells, with a southwestern United States setting, the traditional tale about three billy goat brothers who trick a beast that lives under the bridge.

ISBN-13: 978-0-7614-5343-7

[1. Fairy tales. 2. Folklore—Norway.] I. Gilpin, Stephen, ill. II. Asbjørnsen, Peter Christen, 1812-1885. Tre bukkene Bruse English. III. Title.

PZ8.K527Tgm 2007

398.2—dc22

[E]

2006013122

The text of this book is set in Chalkboard.

The art for this book was drawn with a #2 pencil and colored in Photoshop.

Book design by Vera Soki

Printed in China

First edition

1 3 5 6 4 2

For Blake
—E.A.K.

For Fozzie
—S.G.

Once upon a time three cabritos lived with their mother on a ranch near the Rio Grande. The three cabritos loved to play music. They had their own band.

Reynaldo, the smallest and youngest, played the fiddle.

Orlando, the middle one, played the guitar.

Augustín, the oldest and biggest, played the accordion.

One day the three cabritos heard there was going to be a fiesta just across the border in Mexico.

"Let's go!" the three cabritos said. "There will be singing and dancing and plenty to eat. We'll take our instruments and play all night. We always have a good time when we go to Mexico."

"Don't go!" their mother pleaded. "To get there, you have to cross the bridge over the Rio Grande. You know who lives under that bridge: Chupacabra, the goat-sucker! What if he catches you? You will look like a dead cactus when he is done."

"Don't worry, Mama," said the three cabritos. "We're not afraid of Chupacabra."

"Well, I am," their mother said. "Be careful and have a good time at the fiesta. But I won't rest until you come home."

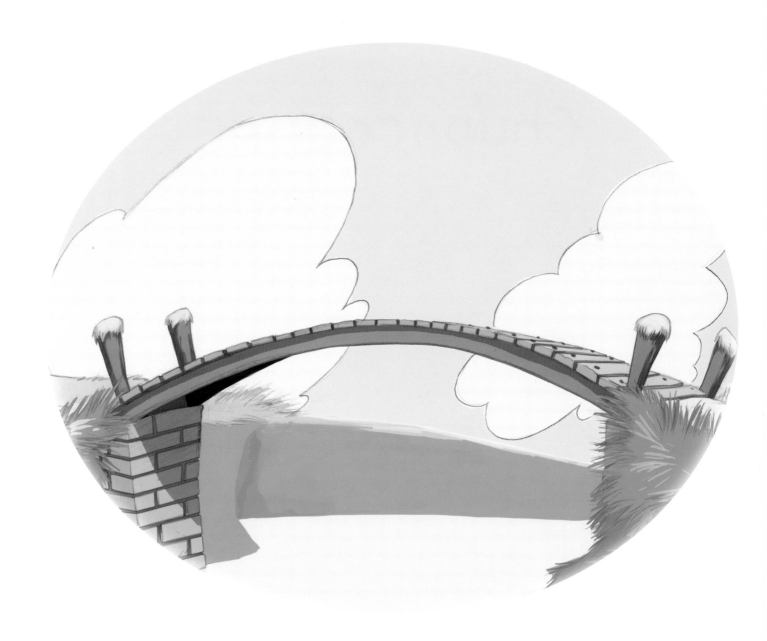

The three cabritos set out for Mexico. Reynaldo walked the fastest. He arrived at the bridge first.

As he crossed, something jumped out from underneath the bridge:

Chupacabra!

"Buenos días, Cabrito," Chupacabra said. "Say your prayers. I'm going to eat you."

"Don't eat me!" Reynaldo pleaded. "I'm so small and thin. My older brother Orlando will be coming along soon. He's much bigger. He'll make a better meal. Let me go, Señor Chupacabra. Please!"

"Maybe I will and maybe I won't," Chupacabra said. "What's that you're carrying under your arm?"

"My fiddle."

"Play something for me. If I like it, I'll let you go and eat your brother instead."

"Gracias, Señor Chupacabra," said Reynaldo. He tuned his fiddle and began to play. Chupacabra danced back and forth across the bridge until he grew tired.

"That's enough. You can go."

Reynaldo took his fiddle and ran across the bridge as fast as he could. He didn't stop until he was well into Mexico.

Orlando came along next. As he was crossing the bridge, Chupacabra leaped out in front of him.

"Buenos días, Cabrito. Say your prayers. I'm going to eat you."

"Don't do that, Señor Chupacabra!" Orlando begged. "I'm so skinny and weak. My older brother, Augustín, is coming along soon. He is big and strong. He'll make a much better meal. Let me go. Please!"

"Maybe I will and maybe I won't," Chupacabra said. "What's that on your back?"

"My guitar."

"Play something for me," Chupacabra said. "If I like it, I'll let you go. I'll eat your brother instead."

"Gracias, Señor Chupacabra!" Orlando tuned his guitar. He began to play. Chupacabra hopped and twirled across the bridge until he grew tired.

"That's enough. You can go," he told Orlando.

Orlando grabbed his guitar and ran across the bridge as fast as he could. He didn't stop until he was miles into Mexico.

Augustín, the last of the three cabritos, arrived at the bridge. Chupacabra jumped up before him.

"Buenos días, Cabrito," Chupacabra said. "Say your prayers. I'm going to eat you."

"Maybe you will and maybe you won't," said Augustín. "I'm a lot bigger and stronger than my brothers."

"You're not bigger or stronger than me!" Chupacabra sneered.

"You're right," Augustín said. "You're going to eat me no matter what I do. May I ask a favor? Let me play my accordion one last time. Then I'll lie down on the bridge, and you can gobble me up."

"Go ahead, Cabrito," said Chupacabra. "Play your accordion. When you're done, I'll eat you."

Augustín began to play. Chupacabra danced and leaped, hopped and twirled, pranced and twisted from one end of the bridge to the other. At last, he cried, "You can stop playing now, Cabrito. I'm getting tired."

"I'm not tired at all," said Augustín. "I forgot to tell you. I have a magic accordion. When I play it, everyone has to keep dancing until I stop."

"Enough, Cabrito! I can't dance anymore!"

"Not yet. I don't want to stop. I'm having a good time."

Augustín began playing faster and faster. Chupacabra whirled around and around. His face turned red. His eyes bulged. Smoke came out of his ears.

"No more, Cabrito!
I beg you!
It
will be
the end of me
if you
don't stop!"

"Is that so?" said Augustín. "Then I'll keep playing." And he did, faster than ever before. Chupacabra gasped and groaned. With a sudden shriek, he fell down on the bridge.

Chupacabra shriveled like a punctured balloon. He grew smaller and smaller until only his husk remained, as dry and brittle as a dead cactus. Augustín crushed it beneath his hooves as he crossed over to Mexico.

The three cabritos played all night at the fiesta.
When they went home in the morning, they crossed
the bridge together. No one had to worry about
Chupacabra anymore.

So they say.

But as for me, whenever I cross over that bridge into Mexico, I make sure to carry my harmonica in my pocket. Just in case.

Author's Note

The Three Cabrito is my own original retelling of "The Three Billy Goats Gruff" with a Texas twist.

Cabrito means "young goat" or "kid" in Spanish. Chupacabra is a legendary creature who attacks farm animals at night. Chupacabra was first reported in Puerto Rico. Subsequent sightings followed in Florida, Texas, and Mexico.

There is absolutely no scientific evidence that Chupacabra exists.

So they say.

Glossary and Pronunciation Guide

Augustín — Ow-goos-TEEN

Buenos días (BWAY-nohs DEE-ahs) — hello, good day

Cabrito (Cah-BREE-toe) — a young goat, a kid

Chupacabra (Chu-pah-CAH-bra) — the "goat-sucker"; a vampire monster

Fiesta (Fee-ES-tah) — a party, festival, celebration

Gracias (GRAH-see-ahs) — thank you

Orlando — Or-LAHN-doe

Reynaldo — Ray-NAHL-doe

Señor (Seh-NYOHR) — mister